FIVE
FAVOURITE
BEDTIME
TALES

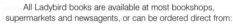

All Ladybird books are available at most bookshops,
supermarkets and newsagents, or can be ordered direct from:
Ladybird Postal Sales
PO Box 133 Paignton TQ3 2YP England
Telephone: (+44) 01803 554761
Fax: (+44) 01803 663394

A catalogue record for this book is available
from the British Library

Published by Ladybird Books Ltd
A subsidiary of the Penguin Group
A Pearson Company
© LADYBIRD BOOKS LTD MCMXCVIII

Stories in this book were previously published by Ladybird Books Ltd
in the *Favourite Tales* series.

LADYBIRD and the device of a Ladybird are trademarks of
Ladybird Books Ltd Loughborough Leicestershire UK

FIVE
FAVOURITE
BEDTIME
TALES

Ladybird

Introduction

Children will treasure this collection of timeless bedtime tales. The easy-to-read retellings, enhanced by exciting, richly colourful illustrations, faithfully capture all the magic of the original stories.

Contents

Hansel and Gretel

Based on the story by
Jacob and Wilhelm Grimm
retold by Audrey Daly
Illustrated by Peter Stevenson

Snow White and the Seven Dwarfs

Based on the story by
Jacob and Wilhelm Grimm
retold by Raymond Sibley
Illustrated by Martin Aitchison

The Ugly Duckling

Based on the story by
Hans Christian Andersen
retold by Lynne Bradbury
Illustrated by Petula Stone

Jack and the Beanstalk

Based on a traditional folk tale
retold by Audrey Daly
Illustrated by Martin Salisbury

Thumbelina

Based on the story by
Hans Christian Andersen
retold by Audrey Daly
Illustrated by Petula Stone

Cover and Borders illustrated by
Peter Stevenson

Hansel
and Gretel

Once upon a time, a boy called Hansel and his sister Gretel lived with their father and stepmother in a cottage near a forest.

They were so poor that they sometimes did not have enough to eat. One day the children heard their stepmother say to their father, "Tomorrow we must take the children deep into the forest and leave them there. Otherwise *we* shall starve."

Gretel was frightened, but Hansel had a plan. That night, when everyone was asleep, he crept outside and filled his pockets with shiny white pebbles.

The next morning, when the family went into the forest, Hansel walked more slowly than the others. When no one was looking, he dropped his pebbles along the path.

As soon as they were deep in the forest, their stepmother left the children by themselves, telling them to wait until someone came to fetch them. They waited until it grew dark, but no one came.

At last the moon rose. Hansel showed Gretel the pebbles he had dropped. They shone white in the moonlight and showed the children the way home.

When the tired, hungry children
arrived back at the cottage, their
father was very glad to see them.

But their stepmother was angry.
Next day she told the woodcutter
that they would have to take the
children into the forest again.

"And this time we must see that they *can't* find their way home!"

That night, when everyone was asleep, Hansel got up to collect some pebbles again. But his stepmother had locked the door and hidden the key. Hansel could not get out.

In the morning, before they all
set off, their stepmother gave
the two children a small piece
of bread each for their lunch.

They hadn't gone very far before
Hansel began to walk more slowly
than the others.

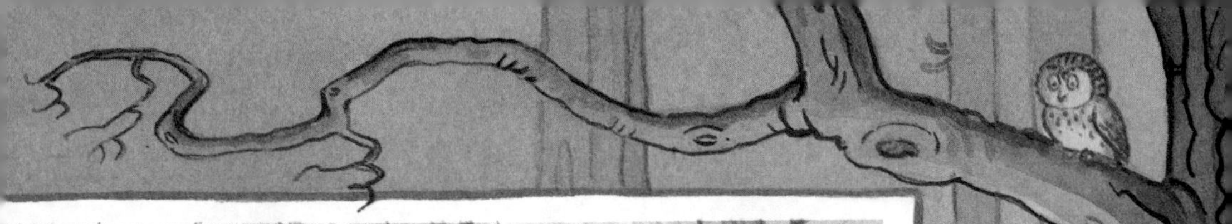

"Why are you so slow?" his
stepmother shouted, looking
back at him. "Hurry up!"

"I'm only saying goodbye to my
friends the birds," said Hansel.
But he was really stopping to drop
breadcrumbs along the path.

When they had gone deep into the forest, the woodcutter lit a small fire for his children. Sadly, he told them to wait beside it until someone came to fetch them.

The children waited until it grew dark, but no one came.

When the moon rose, Hansel and Gretel looked for the trail of breadcrumbs to lead them home.

But there wasn't a single crumb to be seen. The birds had eaten them all!

The children tried to find their way out of the forest, but they didn't know which path to take. They were completely lost.

Hansel and Gretel were tired and frightened and very, very hungry. They had no idea where to go or what to do next.

Suddenly Gretel cried, "Hansel, look!" Just ahead of them was a strange little house made of cakes and gingerbread, with a roof of sugary icing.

Laughing with pleasure, the children broke off bits of the house and began to eat.

Suddenly the door of the little house creaked open. An old woman looked out.

"Hello, children," she said, smiling. "Come inside, and I will give you food and somewhere warm to sleep."

The children went into the house, and she gave them some delicious pancakes and milk. In the back room there were two little beds.

Hansel and Gretel were happy to be safe at last with such a kind woman. They didn't know that she was really a wicked witch who liked to eat little children!

Next day the witch put Gretel to
work scrubbing the floors. Then
she took poor Hansel and locked
him in a cage. "I'm going to fatten
you up and eat you!" she cackled.
"I'm looking forward to that!"

Every morning the witch, who had
very poor eyesight, told Hansel to
hold out his finger so that she
could feel how fat he had grown.

But each time clever Hansel held
out a chicken bone instead.

"Not nearly fat enough yet," the
witch would mutter.

Days went by, and Hansel kept holding out a chicken bone instead of his finger.

At last the witch grew impatient. "I'm not waiting any longer! He *must* be fat enough by now," she said one morning. "Today I'm going to cook Hansel and eat him. Gretel, light the oven."

With tears in her eyes, Gretel did as she was told.

"Now, climb in and see if the oven is hot," the witch ordered.

But Gretel was sure that the witch was trying to trick her. "I can't climb into the oven," she said. "I'm much too big."

"Of course you can," said the witch angrily. "Look, I'll show you." And she bent down and stuck her head in the oven.

Gretel didn't waste a second. She gave the witch a hard push and slammed the door. The witch screamed with rage, but she couldn't get out.

When Gretel was sure the witch
was dead, she unlocked Hansel's
cage and let her brother out.

"We're free!" she cried. "We can
go home now!"

But first Hansel and Gretel searched the witch's house from top to bottom. In the attic, they were amazed to find chests full of pearls and rubies and diamonds.

"We must take some of these home to Father," said Hansel.

As the children set off, Hansel saw a white dove flying high above. "It's one of my friends showing us the way!" he said.

Soon the children saw their own cottage through the trees. Their father was overjoyed to see them.

"Your stepmother has gone, and she is never coming back," he said, hugging the children.

When he saw the jewels, the woodcutter couldn't believe his eyes. "We're rich!" he cried. "And we shall never be parted again."

And they never were.

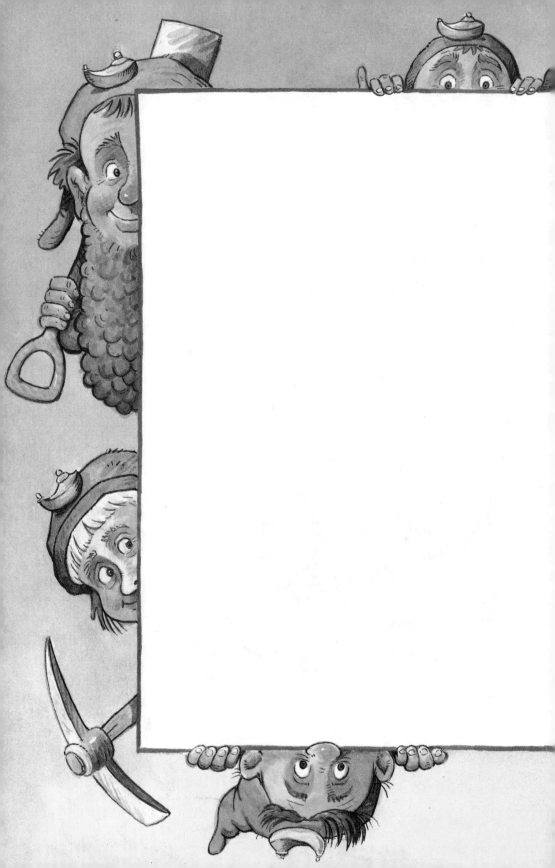

Snow White
and the Seven Dwarfs

One snowy day, a queen sat sewing at her window. As she glanced through the black ebony window frame, she pricked her finger and three small drops of blood fell upon her sewing.

The Queen sighed. "I wish I had a baby girl with cheeks as red as blood, skin as white as snow and hair as black as ebony," she said.

Soon afterwards, her wish came true.
She had a lovely baby daughter with
red cheeks, white skin and black hair.
She named the baby Snow White.

But before long the Queen died, and
Snow White's father married again.

The new Queen was beautiful, but she
was vain and
selfish too.
Her dearest
possession was
a magic
mirror.

Every day the Queen would stand in front of her mirror and ask,

"Mirror, mirror, on the wall,
Who is the fairest of us all?"

And the mirror would reply,

"Thou, O Queen, art the fairest of all!"

But Snow White was growing up and becoming more lovely every day.

One day, when the Queen asked,

*"Mirror, mirror, on the wall,
Who is the fairest of us all?"*

the mirror gave a new reply.

"O Queen, Snow White is fairest of all!"

The Queen grew pale with rage.

From that day on, the Queen hated Snow White with all her heart. Every day the girl grew more and more beautiful. In her fury, the Queen sent for a huntsman.

"Take Snow White into the forest," she ordered. "Kill her and bring her heart back to me."

So the huntsman took Snow White into the forest, but he could not kill the lovely girl. "Run," he said gruffly, "and never return!"

Snow White was lost and frightened. "Oh where shall I go?" she wept. At last she glimpsed a little cottage in a clearing.

Cold and tired, Snow White peeped inside. What an odd little place it was! There were seven tiny chairs and seven tiny plates. Along one wall, there were seven little beds.

As there was no one about, Snow White lay down on one of the beds and fell fast asleep.

Unknown to the sleeping girl, the cottage belonged to seven dwarfs, who worked in the mines all day. At nightfall, they came home from their work and lit seven candles.

"Goodness me, there's someone here!" cried one of the dwarfs in surprise, when he saw Snow White.

The noise woke Snow White, and the seven little dwarfs crowded round her. "How beautiful she is!" they cried.

"Why have you come here, my dear, and how can we help you?" asked one of the dwarfs in a gentle voice.

Snow White explained about the wicked Queen. As she told her story, she grew so sad that she began to cry.

"Hush, my dear," said the kind little men. "You can live here with us, safe from that evil woman." Snow White gratefully accepted their offer.

In the palace, the Queen once again stood before her magic mirror. She did not know that the huntsman had disobeyed her and brought her an animal's heart instead of Snow White's.

Rubbing her hands with glee, the
Queen smiled and said,

"Mirror, mirror, on the wall,
Who is the fairest of us all?"

And the mirror replied,

"O Queen, Snow White is fairest of all.
For in the forest,
where seven dwarfs dwell,
Snow White is still
alive and well."

Screaming with rage, the Queen
planned her revenge.

Next morning, after the dwarfs left for work, Snow White sang happily to herself as she tidied the little house.

Before long an old pedlar woman knocked at the door. It was the Queen in disguise. "Come and look at these pretty things, dear child," she cackled.

Snow White was enchanted.

She let the old woman tie a pink velvet ribbon around her neck to see how it would look. Suddenly, the old woman pulled the ribbon tight! Snow White fell to the ground.

The dwarfs found Snow White lying close to death. They untied the ribbon so she could breathe, and by the next morning she was well again.

"That pedlar was the wicked Queen!" said the dwarfs. Before they left for work, they made Snow White promise never to open the door to anyone.

Meanwhile, once again, the magic mirror had told the wicked Queen that Snow White was not dead.

The angry Queen disguised herself as
a kind old lady selling combs. Again,
Snow White nearly died, for the
combs were poisoned.

This time the dwarfs were very cross. "Do not let *anyone* into the house," they said firmly.

When the mirror told the Queen that she had failed again, she was furious. She was determined that Snow White should die.

Next day the Queen took a basket of poisoned apples and tapped on the cottage window.

"I don't need to come in," she said cunningly, "but do try this lovely apple, dear child. It's delicious!"

Snow White could see no harm in a shiny red apple, so she took a big bite.

When the dwarfs came home, they found Snow White lifeless on the floor. They did everything they could to save her, but it was no use. She lay cold and still.

"We have lost the loveliest girl that ever lived," they sobbed.

Far away in the palace, the Queen
stood proudly before her mirror.

"Mirror, mirror, on the wall,
Who is the fairest of us all?"

And the mirror answered at last,

"Thou, O Queen, art the fairest of all."

The dwarfs could not bear to part with Snow White. Her cheeks were still as red as blood, her skin was as white as snow and her hair was as black as ebony.

So the little men made a glass coffin and laid Snow White's body tenderly in it. She looked for all the world as though she were only sleeping.

Day and night, the dwarfs kept watch beside the coffin. One evening, a young prince rode by.

As soon as he saw Snow White, he fell in love with her. "I beg you to let me take her home with me," he said, "so that she can lie in a palace as she deserves."

At long last, the dwarfs agreed.

As the Prince's servants were carrying the coffin down the mountain, they stumbled. Suddenly a piece of apple, which had been caught in Snow White's throat, fell out!

Snow White opened her eyes and saw the handsome Prince. "I love you," he whispered. "Please say that you will marry me." Snow White smiled happily.

The dwarfs, overjoyed that their
beloved Snow White was alive, waved
goodbye as she rode off with the
Prince.

Soon Snow White and her prince
were married. They lived happily ever
after – and the wicked Queen and her
mirror were never heard of again!

The Ugly
Duckling

It was summer in the country. All the hay had been stacked, and the fields of wheat were yellow. Tall dock leaves grew on the banks of the canals.

Among the dock leaves, on her nest, sat a duck waiting for her eggs to hatch. She had been waiting for a long time.

At last the eggs began to crack and,
one by one, the ducklings
poked their heads out.

Before long, all the eggs had hatched except the biggest one. The duck sat a little longer, until out tumbled the last of her chicks.

But when she looked at him, she said, "Oh, dear! You're so big and ugly."

The next day was warm and sunny, so the duck took her new family down to the canal. She splashed into the water and, one by one, her ducklings followed her. Soon all of them were swimming beautifully, even the ugly grey one.

Next the ducklings went into the duck yard. "Stay close to me," warned their mother. The other ducks thought the ducklings were beautiful – all except the big ugly one.

The ducklings stayed in the duck yard.
But the ugly duckling was very unhappy
there. The older ducks pecked at him
and laughed. He had nowhere to hide,
so one day he ran away.

He ran and ran until he came to the
great marsh where the wild ducks
lived. There he lay in the rushes for
two whole weeks.

Then some wild ducks and some geese came to look at him. "You're *very* ugly," they said, and they laughed at him.

The poor little ugly duckling ran away from the great marsh. He ran and ran over fields and meadows. The wind blew and the rain rained. The duckling was cold, wet and very tired.

Just as it was getting dark, the duckling found a little cottage.

The cottage was very old and the door was falling off. This left a gap just big enough for the duckling to creep inside, out of the cold.

An old woman lived there. She had a cat that purred and a hen that laid eggs. She found the cold, starving little duckling in the morning.

The old woman looked at the
duckling and said, "You can stay.
Now we shall have duck eggs
to eat, too!"

So the duckling stayed. But he *didn't*
lay eggs.

The cat said to him, "Can you purr?"

"No," said the duckling.

The hen asked, "Can you lay eggs?"

"No," said the duckling, sadly.

"Then you must go,"
said the cat and
the hen.

So the ugly duckling was alone once again. He walked in the marshes and floated on the water, and everywhere he went, all the birds and animals said, "How big and *ugly* you are."

Winter was coming. The leaves began to fall from the trees, and the ground was cold and hard.

The duckling had nowhere to stay.

One evening a flock of birds flew overhead. They were beautiful white swans with long necks.

"I wish *I* was like that," the duckling said sadly to himself.

He travelled on and on and the winter grew colder.

The ground froze and the duckling couldn't find food. One night, as he was pecking to find water, he was so tired that he fell asleep on the ice.

The next morning a farmer found the duckling and took him home so that his wife could take care of him.

As the duckling grew stronger, the farmer's children wanted to play with him. But the children were rough, and the duckling was frightened when they chased him. As soon as he could, he ran away again.

At last the duckling found a safe
hiding place among the reeds in the
marsh. There he stayed for the rest of
the winter.

Then, after many long weeks, the
warm spring sun began to shine again.
The duckling spread his wings – they
were strong wings now. Suddenly he
rose from the ground and flew high
into the air.

Down below, three beautiful swans were swimming on the canal. The duckling flew down to look at them. As he landed, the lonely bird saw his own reflection in the water.

He wasn't an ugly duckling at all! During the long winter he had grown into a beautiful white swan.

The other swans looked at him and admired his grace and beauty. "Come with us," they said.

And he did!

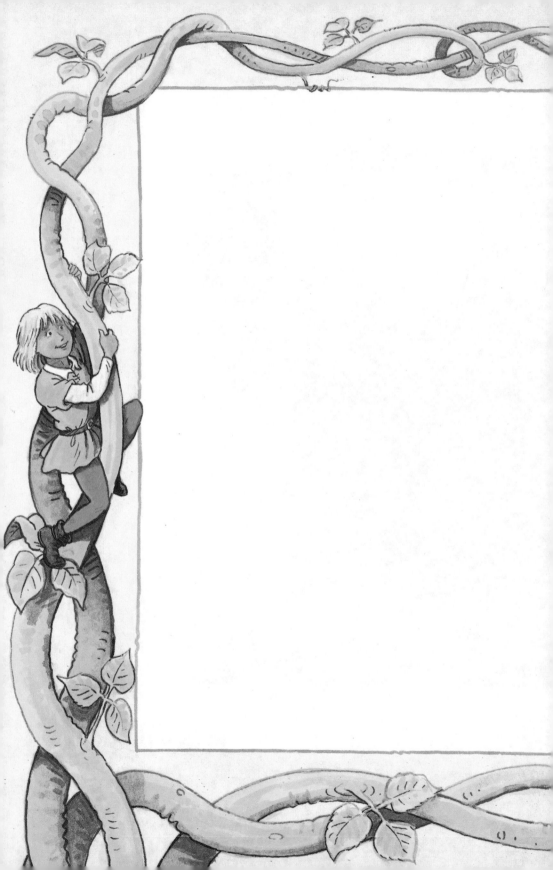

Jack and the Beanstalk

Once upon a time a boy named Jack lived with his mother. All they had in the world was one cow.

One day Jack's mother said, "We have no money for food. We shall have to sell the cow."

So Jack took the cow to market.
On the way, he met a man.

"If you give me your cow," said the
man, "I'll give you some magic beans
that are better than money."

Jack thought the magic beans sounded wonderful, so he gave the man the cow. Then he ran home as fast as he could.

"How much money did you get for the cow?" asked his mother.

"I got something much better than money," said Jack, showing her the magic beans.

"These beans are no good to us!" cried his mother angrily. And she threw them out of the window.

When Jack woke up the next day, his room seemed darker than usual. He went to the window and saw that a huge beanstalk had grown up in the garden overnight.

"I must find out what's at the top," he cried, rushing outside. And he began to climb the beanstalk.

Up and up he climbed. At last he found himself in a bare, rocky wilderness.

There were no plants or animals to be seen anywhere. But a long road led into the distance, and Jack began to walk along it. Towards evening he came to a castle and knocked loudly on the door.

"Could you give me some food and a bed for the night, please?" Jack asked the woman who answered.

"Oh no," said the woman. "My husband is a fierce giant who hates strangers." But Jack begged so hard that she let him in and gave him some supper.

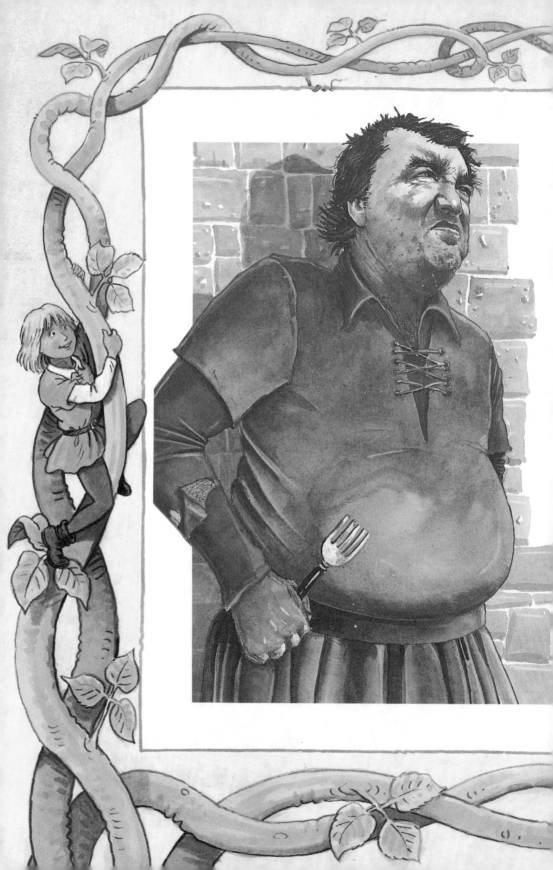

Just as Jack was enjoying some hot soup, he heard the giant coming. The woman quickly hid Jack in a cupboard.

The giant stalked in and roared,

"Fee, fie, foe, fum,
I smell the blood of an Englishman!
Be he alive or be he dead,
I'll grind his bones to make my bread!"

"Nonsense!" said his wife. "There's no one here." And she gave the giant his supper.

When he had finished his supper, the giant bellowed, "Bring me my hen!"

His wife brought a little hen and put it on the table.

"Lay!" shouted the giant.

Jack peeped out of his hiding place.
To his amazement, every time the
giant shouted, the hen laid a little
golden egg.

When he had twelve golden eggs, the
giant fell asleep.

As soon as all was quiet, Jack crept out of the cupboard, grabbed the little hen and tiptoed out.

Then he ran and ran until he was back at the top of the beanstalk. Quickly, he climbed down and took the magic hen to his mother.

How pleased she was! "Long ago, a wicked giant stole this hen from your father," she said. "Now that we have her back, our worries are over."

Jack lived happily with his mother for a while. But he longed for adventure, and one day he decided to climb the beanstalk again.

Just as before, Jack reached the castle towards evening. And once again the giant's wife hid him when they heard the giant roar,

"Fee, fie, foe, fum,
I smell the blood of an Englishman!
Be he alive or be he dead,
I'll grind his bones to make my bread!"

After supper the giant shouted, "Fetch me my money bags!" His wife brought him some sacks filled with gold coins.

The giant emptied the sacks onto the table and counted the coins over and over again. At last he put the money back in the sacks and fell asleep.

Quick as a flash, Jack took the money and ran all the way home.

His mother was delighted when she saw the money bags. "The giant stole this money from your father," she said. "You have done well to bring it back."

Although Jack and his mother were now rich, Jack wanted to climb the beanstalk one last time.

Everything happened just as before.

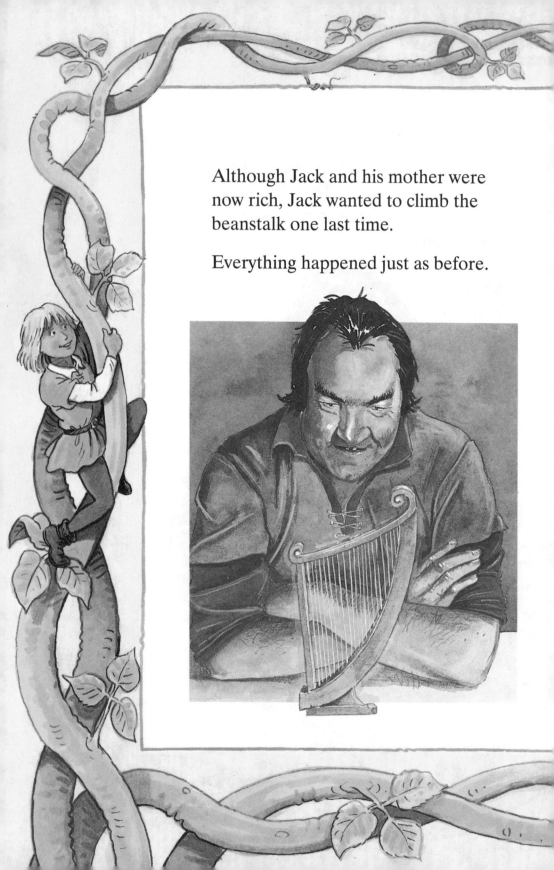

This time the giant's wife brought a beautiful golden harp. "Play!" roared the giant, and the harp began to play soft music.

The music was so gentle that it sent the giant to sleep. But when Jack crept out and seized it, the harp cried, "Master! Master!"

The giant woke up in a rage, just in time to see Jack disappearing through the door with the harp. "Stop, thief!" the giant roared.

Now Jack had to run for his life. The giant took huge strides and was soon hard on Jack's heels. Scrambling down the beanstalk, Jack shouted as loudly as he could, "Mother, Mother, bring the axe!"

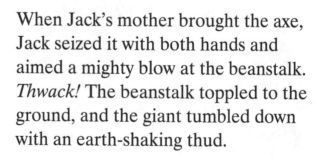

When Jack's mother brought the axe, Jack seized it with both hands and aimed a mighty blow at the beanstalk. *Thwack!* The beanstalk toppled to the ground, and the giant tumbled down with an earth-shaking thud.

So that was the end of the giant.
Jack and his mother were never poor
again, and they both lived happily
ever after.

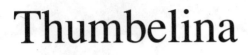

Thumbelina

Once upon a time there was a woman who longed to have a little girl of her own to love and care for. As time passed, and she had no children, she became very sad.

Then one day she heard of a wise old woman who could help, and she went to see her.

The wise old woman smiled. "Take this tiny seed and plant it in a flower pot," she said, "and you will have your little girl."

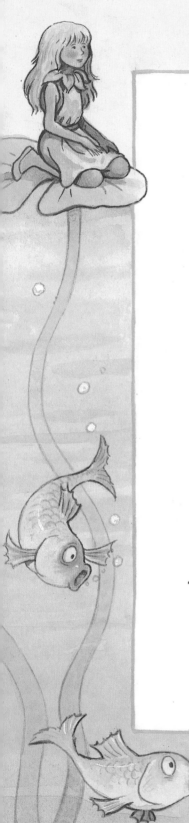

The woman took the seed home and planted it. Soon green shoots appeared, and a flower bud grew between them.

At last the bud opened out into a beautiful yellow flower. And right in the centre was a little girl, no bigger than the woman's thumb.

The woman looked down at the girl. "How pretty you are!" she said. "You are so small and dainty, I'm going to call you Thumbelina."

The woman was happy to have a little girl at last, and she took good care of Thumbelina.

Thumbelina was happy too. She sang songs in her soft, clear voice as she played on the kitchen table. At night she slept in a bed made from a tiny walnut shell.

Then one day a big toad heard
Thumbelina's singing and hopped in
through the window. "What a pretty
wife you would make for my son!" she
said. And she carried Thumbelina
away to the stream where she lived.

The toad left the tiny girl all alone on a lily leaf and went off to find her son.

Thumbelina didn't want to marry an ugly toad at all, but she didn't know how she could escape.

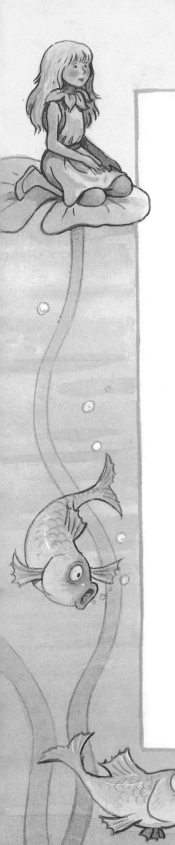

After a while some friendly fish came swimming by. "Please help me," Thumbelina begged. "The toad wants me to marry her son. I must find a way to escape!"

All the fish felt very sorry for Thumbelina. So they spent the whole day nibbling through the stem of the lily leaf, and at last Thumbelina was able to float away.

As she drifted down the stream, Thumbelina met a beautiful butterfly. It took her to a pleasant wood where she could make a home for herself.

Thumbelina was happy in the wood, eating the nuts and berries that she found, and playing with her friends the butterflies.

But soon the days grew colder. When winter came, it was harder for Thumbelina to find food. Her friends the butterflies disappeared, and she was alone.

Then one day Thumbelina met a friendly fieldmouse who was just going into her little house.

"I'm so hungry," Thumbelina said. "Please can you help me?"

The fieldmouse took pity on the girl. "Of course," she said. "You can stay with me in my warm house and share my food."

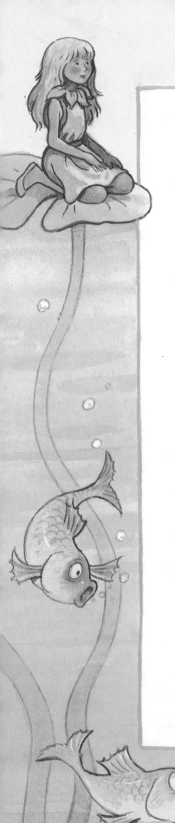

Thumbelina lived happily with the fieldmouse for a long time. But one day the fieldmouse said, "I can't keep you here much longer. Why don't you marry my friend the mole, who lives next door? He has a much bigger house than mine. And he will look after you next winter."

Thumbelina did not want to marry the mole. He lived under the ground and knew nothing of the sunny world outside.

Next day the mole visited Thumbelina. "Please come and see where I live," he said.

Thumbelina did not want to hurt the mole's feelings, so she followed him into the tunnel that led to his dark underground home.

"Be careful," said the mole. "There is a dead bird just here."

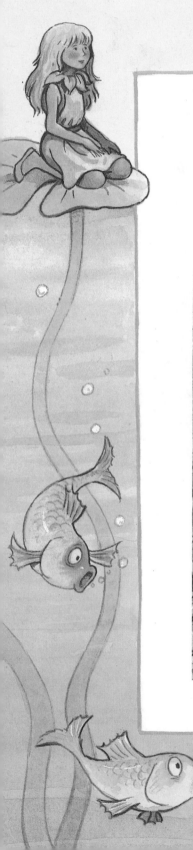

Thumbelina saw that the bird was a swallow. He was not dead, just very cold and weak.

Thumbelina felt sorry for the swallow.
She covered him with dried leaves
and grass to keep him warm.

Thumbelina looked after the swallow
all through the long, cold winter. By
summer he was strong and well and
ready to go back to his own home.

Thumbelina said goodbye to the
swallow as he flew off with his friends.
She was happy that he was well,
but she knew that she would miss
him. And she was sad to think that
before the next winter came, she
would have to marry the mole and live
underground.

When summer ended, Thumbelina looked up at the sky for the last time with tears in her eyes. Birds were flying high overhead, and suddenly one of them swooped down to her. It was the swallow she had saved!

"I am going to a warm country," he told her. "Come with me."

Thumbelina was overjoyed. She climbed onto the swallow's back and flew with him to a faraway land where it was always summer.

This land was full of flowers. And inside every one lived a tiny person, just like Thumbelina!

"We are the Flower People," they said, "and this is your true home. We will call you Maia."

Maia loved her new home. Before long, she married the handsome Prince of the Flower People, and they lived happily ever after.